ALLOSAURUS

CORYTHOSAURUS

PTERANODON

APATOSAURUS

DIMETRODON

ANKYLOSAURUS

TRACHODON

TYRANNOSAURUS REX

STEGOSAURUS

TRICERATOPS

JANE YOLEN

How Do Dinosaurs

Say Good Night?

Illustrated by

MARK TEAGUE

THE BLUE SKY PRESS

An Imprint of Scholastic Inc. · New York

THE BLUE SKY PRESS

Text copyright © 2000 by Jane Yolen

Illustrations copyright © 2000 by Mark Teague

All rights reserved.

Library of Congress card catalog number: 98-56134

ISBN-13: 978-0-545-02737-3

ISBN-10: 0-545-02737-3

12 11 10 9 8 7 6 5 4 3 2 1   07 08 09 10 11

Printed in Singapore   46

This edition first printing, June 2007

For my own little dinosaurs at bedtime:

Maddison Jane and Alison Isabelle

J. Y.

To Mom and Dad

M. T.

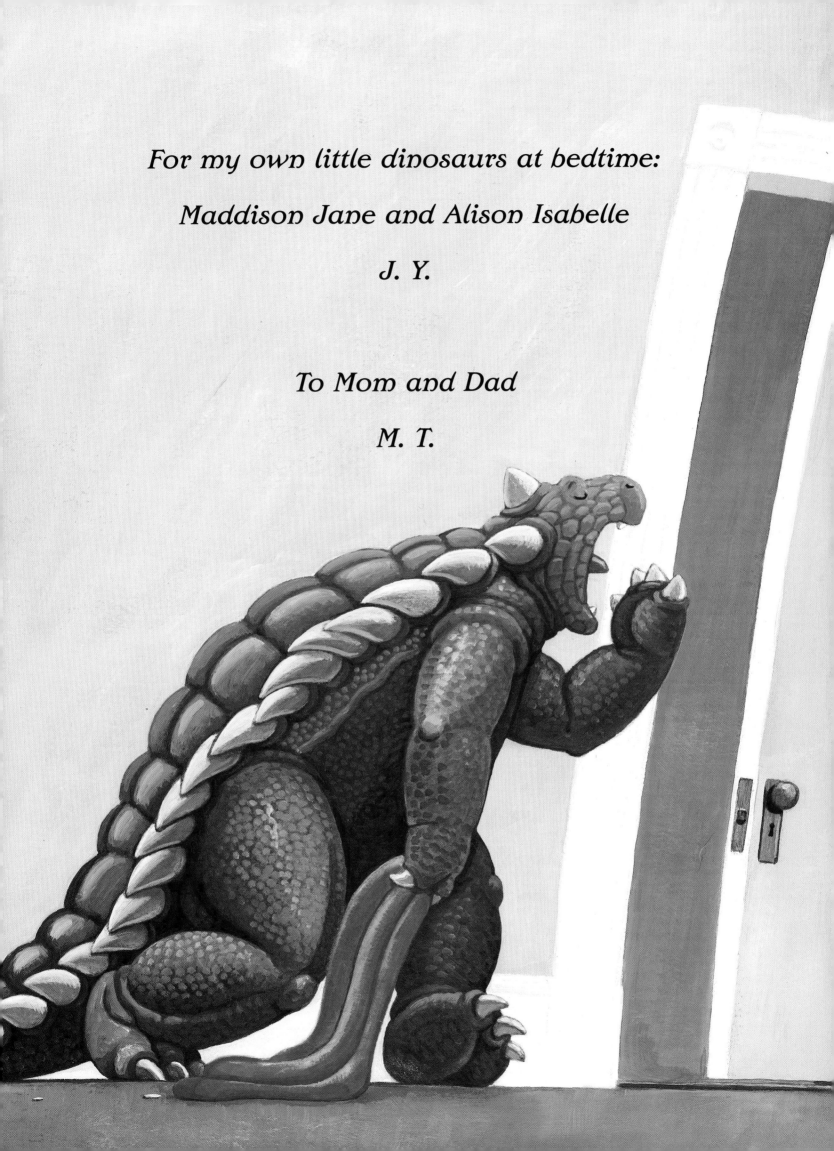

How does
a dinosaur say
good night
when Papa
comes in
to turn off
the light?

Does
a dinosaur
slam
his tail
and pout?

Does he throw
his teddy bear
all about?

Does a
dinosaur
stomp
his feet
on the floor

and shout: "I want to hear one book more!"?

DOES

A DINOSAUR

ROAR?

How does a dinosaur say good night
when *Mama* comes in
to turn off the light?

Does he swing his neck

from side to side?

Does he up
and demand
a piggyback ride?

ANKYLOSAURUS

Does he mope,
does he moan,
does he sulk,
does he sigh?

Does he fall on the top
of his covers and cry?

No, dinosaurs don't.
They don't even try.

They give
a big kiss.

They turn out
the light.

DIMETRODON

They tuck in
their tails.
They whisper,
"Good night!"

They give
a big hug,
then give
one kiss
more.

Good night.

Good night, little dinosaur.

ALLOSAURUS

CORYTHOSAURUS

PTERANODON

APATOSAURUS

DIMETRODON

ANKYLOSAURUS

TRACHODON

TYRANNOSAURUS REX

STEGOSAURUS

TRICERATOPS